ROALD DAHL

MISCHIEF AND MAYHEM

Illustrated by Quentin Blake

Compiled by
Kay Woodward

PUFFIN

PUFFIN BOOKS

UK | USA | Canada | Ireland | Australia
India | New Zealand | South Africa

Puffin Books is part of the Penguin Random House group of companies
whose addresses can be found at global.penguinrandomhouse.com.

www.penguin.co.uk
www.puffin.co.uk
www.ladybird.co.uk

Extracts taken from: *James and the Giant Peach* first published 1961; *Matilda* first published 1988;
Charlie and the Chocolate Factory first published 1964; *Boy* first published 1984;
The Wonderful Story of Henry Sugar and Six More first published 1977; *The BFG* first published 1982;
The Enormous Crocodile first published 1978; *George's Marvellous Medicine* first published 1981;
Danny the Champion of the World first published 1975; *The Witches* first published 1983;
Fantastic Mr Fox first published 1970; *Revolting Rhymes* first published 1982;
The Twits first published 1980; *Charlie and the Great Glass Elevator* first published 1972

First published 2013
This abridged edition 2016
001

Text copyright © Roald Dahl Nominee Ltd, 2013
Illustrations copyright © Quentin Blake, 2013
Text design by Mandy Norman

The moral right of the author and illustrator has been asserted

Set in Baskerville and Amasis
Printed in Great Britain by Clays Ltd, St Ives plc

A CIP catalogue record for this book is available from the British Library

ISBN: 978-0-141-37796-4

All correspondence to
Puffin Books
Penguin Random House Children's
80 Strand, London WC2R 0RL

www.greenpenguin.co.uk

Introduction

STOP!

Yes, you. Stop right there. Don't move.
Are you an adult? Oh, dear. I'm sorry. This book
is absolutely **NOT** meant for you. Kindly close
the pages and go and do something grown-up
instead. (Perhaps you could make a roast dinner
with a hundred vegetables or creosote a fence or
something.) Off you go. Have they gone? Good.
Hello, non-adult! This book is meant for **YOU**.
But be warned. It contains **mischief** and
mayhem of such extreme naughtiness that you
will need the cunning of Fantastic Mr Fox and the
cleverness of Matilda to continue. *You're* cunning
AND clever? Excellent. We'll get along just fine.
Now, read on.

If you've bought, borrowed or been given this **TRULY NAUGHTY** book, then you surely already know of Roald Dahl. But, just in case you're one of the 27 people on the planet who haven't heard of him, let me tell you a little more.

ROALD DAHL *was* ONE *of* THE BEST STORYTELLERS EVER.

There. Done. I beg your pardon? You'd like to know even more than that? Well, why didn't you say so?

Roald Dahl was born in Wales in 1916 to Norwegian parents. He had four sisters. Sadly, both his father and his eldest sister died when he was very young. And then when he wasn't much older – just nine years old – his mother sent him away to boarding school in England. Roald Dahl hated it so much that he pretended to have appendicitis so that he would be sent home. He *was* sent home.

Hurray!

But when he was found out he was sent back to school again.

Boo.

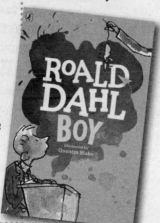

In between detention and homework and being achingly homesick, Roald spent the rest of his school years trying to outwit his **VERY STRICT** teachers and the **FORMIDABLE** matron. And testing new chocolate bars for a **VERY FAMOUS** chocolate company. Luckily, he also loved making up stories. (He wrote it all down in a book called *Boy*, if you'd like to find out EVEN MORE.)

The rest of Roald Dahl's life is like something out of a storybook too. He worked in London, which was chilly, and Africa, which wasn't. He flew fighter-planes in the Second World War, which was very scary. (Unfortunately, he crashed one in the desert, which was even scarier.) He was a spy. Shhhh. And THEN he became a writer. **Phew.**

Roald Dahl wrote stories that were funny and amazing and scary and sad. There were **unlikely heroes** and **fearsome villains**. There were funny bits and not-so-funny bits and buckets and buckets of **MISCHIEF. And MAYHEM.** Don't forget the mayhem. Was it his time at boarding school that turned him into a trickster? Was it his fabulously dark sense of humour? Was it just because he liked making people laugh? Who knows? **Roald Dahl, that's who.**

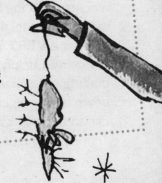

PS The tricks and pranks and japes and jokes and jests and stunts in this book have been given a star rating to indicate the level of difficulty.

One-star tricks are for **total beginners** in the art of trickery.

Two-star tricks are for more **experienced tricksters** and pranksters.

Three-star tricks should only be attempted by magicians, conjurers, professional jokers, astrophysicists or **senior members of MI6 and the FBI**. Approach with caution (and a member of the armed services, if you have one handy).

In which James and his friends trick a flock of seagulls into giving them a lift.

In a few minutes everything was ready.

It was very quiet now on the top of the peach. There was nobody in sight – nobody except the Earthworm.

One half of the Earthworm, looking like a great, thick, juicy, pink sausage, lay innocently in the sun for all the seagulls to see.

The other half of him was dangling down the tunnel.

James was crouching close beside the Earthworm in the tunnel entrance, just below the surface, waiting for the first seagull. He had a loop of silk string in his hands.

The Old-Green-Grasshopper and the Ladybird were further down the tunnel, holding on to the Earthworm's tail, ready to pull him quickly in out of danger as soon as James gave the word.

And far below, in the great stone of the peach, the Glow-worm was lighting up the room so that the two spinners, the Silkworm and Miss Spider, could see what they were doing. The Centipede was down there too, exhorting them both frantically to greater efforts, and every now and again James could hear his voice coming up faintly from the depths, shouting, 'Spin, Silkworm, spin, you great fat lazy brute! Faster, faster, or we'll throw you to the sharks!'

'Here comes the first seagull!' whispered James. 'Keep still now, Earthworm. Keep still. The rest of you get ready to pull.'

'Please don't let it spike me,' begged the Earthworm.

'I won't, I won't. Ssshh . . .'

Out of the corner of one eye, James watched the seagull as it came swooping down towards the Earthworm. And then suddenly it was so close that he could see its small black eyes and its curved beak, and the beak was open, ready to grab a nice piece of flesh out of the Earthworm's back.

'Pull!' shouted James.

The Old-Green-Grasshopper and the Ladybird gave the Earthworm's tail an enormous tug, and like magic the Earthworm disappeared into the tunnel. At the same time, up went James's hand and the seagull flew right into the loop of silk that he was holding out. The loop, which had been cleverly made, tightened just the right amount (but not too much) around its neck, and the seagull was captured.

'Hooray!' shouted the Old-Green-Grasshopper, peering out of the tunnel. 'Well done, James!'

Up flew the seagull with James paying out the silk string as it went. He gave it about fifty yards and then tied the string to the stem of the peach.

'Next one!' he shouted, jumping back into the tunnel. 'Up you get again, Earthworm! Bring up some more silk, Centipede!'

'Oh, I don't like this at all,' wailed the Earthworm. 'It only just missed me! I even felt the wind on my back as it went swishing past!'

'Ssshh!' whispered James. 'Keep still! Here comes another one!'

So they did it again.

And again, and again, and again.

And the seagulls kept coming, and James caught them one after the other and tethered them to the peach stem.

'One hundred seagulls!' he shouted, wiping the sweat from his face.

'Keep going!' they cried. 'Keep going, James!'

'Two hundred seagulls!'

'Three hundred seagulls!'

'Four hundred seagulls!'

The sharks, as though sensing that they were in danger of losing their prey, were hurling themselves at the peach more furiously than ever, and the peach was sinking lower and lower still in the water.

'Five hundred seagulls!' James shouted.

'Silkworm says she's running out of silk!' yelled the Centipede from below. 'She says she can't keep it up much longer. Nor can Miss Spider!'

'Tell them they've *got* to!' James answered. 'They can't stop now!'

'We're lifting!' somebody shouted.

'No, we're not!'

'I felt it!'

'Put on another seagull, quick!'

'Quiet, everybody! Quiet! Here's one coming now!'

This was the five hundred and first seagull, and the moment that James caught it and tethered it to the stem with all the others, the whole enormous peach suddenly started rising up slowly out of the water.

'Look out! Here we go! Hold on, boys!'

But then it stopped.

And there it hung.

It hovered and swayed, but it went no higher.

The bottom of it was just touching the water. It was like a delicately balanced scale that needed only the tiniest push to tip it one way or the other.

'One more will do it!' shouted the Old-Green-Grasshopper, looking out of the tunnel. 'We're almost there!'

And now came the big moment. Quickly, the five hundred and second seagull was caught and harnessed to the peach-stem . . .

And then suddenly . . .

But slowly . . .

Majestically . . .

Like some fabulous golden balloon . . .

With all the seagulls straining at the strings above . . .

The giant peach rose up dripping out of the water and began climbing towards the heavens.

But don't do that, do THIS!

TRICK

The Booby-trapped Peach

Unless you happen to have a giant-fruit-and-veg shop nearby, you're unlikely to have a giant peach. (Or a giant earthworm, for that matter.) **DON'T PANIC**. For this trick, you will need one average, run-of-the-mill, really quite normal-sized peach, available from all good fruit-and-veg shops. But it must be VERY RIPE.

Why did the peach stop at the top of the hill? **Because it ran out of juice.**

YOU WILL NEED:

☆ One ripe peach
☆ One jelly worm (the edible sort)
☆ One cocktail stick or a toothpick
☆ One fruit bowl

WHAT YOU DO:

1. Being VERY careful, **spear your peach** with a cocktail stick or toothpick and wiggle it about a bit so that you've made a small tunnel in your sticky, juicy fruit.

2. **Poke the jelly worm into the tunnel**. Leave a little bit of the worm sticking out of the peach, just like in *James and the Giant Peach*.

3. Put the **booby-trapped peach** into the fruit bowl.

4. # Wait.

5. If a grown-up does not immediately decide that they would like to sink their teeth into a delicious peach then you may have to **fill their heads with fruity, sticky, juicy thoughts** until they can stand it no longer and simply have to eat a peach RIGHT NOW.

6. Get ready to double up with laughter when the grown-up bites into the ripe peach and thinks they have eaten **A REAL LIVE EARTHWORM**.

7. **Double up with laughter. Or run.**

From Matilda

The Platinum-Blond Man

In which Matilda swaps OIL OF VIOLETS HAIR TONIC for PLATINUM BLONDE HAIR-DYE EXTRA STRONG and makes her father see RED. Actually, yellow. Hmm. Blond, really.

Mr Wormwood kept his hair looking bright and strong, or so he thought, by rubbing into it every morning large quantities of a lotion called OIL OF VIOLETS HAIR TONIC. A bottle of this smelly purple mixture always stood on the shelf above the sink in the bathroom alongside all the toothbrushes, and a very vigorous scalp massage with OIL OF VIOLETS took place daily after shaving was completed. This hair and scalp massage was always accompanied by loud masculine grunts and heavy breathing and gasps of 'Ahhh, that's better! That's the stuff! Rub it right into the roots!' which could be clearly heard by Matilda in her bedroom across the corridor.

Now, in the early morning privacy of the bathroom, Matilda unscrewed the cap of her father's OIL OF VIOLETS and tipped three-quarters of the contents down the drain. Then she filled the bottle up with her mother's PLATINUM BLONDE HAIR-DYE EXTRA STRONG. She carefully left enough of her father's original hair tonic in the bottle so that when she gave it a good shake the whole thing still looked reasonably purple. She then replaced the bottle on the shelf above the sink, taking care to put her mother's bottle back in the cupboard. So far so good.

At breakfast time Matilda sat quietly at the dining-room table eating her cornflakes. Her brother sat opposite her with his back to the door devouring hunks of bread smothered with a mixture of peanut-butter and strawberry jam. The mother was just out of sight around the corner in the kitchen making Mr

Wormwood's breakfast which always had to be two fried eggs on fried bread with three pork sausages and three strips of bacon and some fried tomatoes.

At this point Mr Wormwood came noisily into the room. He was incapable of entering any room quietly, especially at breakfast time. He always had to make his appearance felt immediately by creating a lot of noise and clatter. One could almost hear him saying, 'It's me! Here I come, the great man himself, the master of the house, the wage-earner, the one who makes it possible for all the rest of you to live so well! Notice me and pay your respects!'

On this occasion he strode in and slapped his son on the back and shouted, 'Well, my boy, your father feels he's in for another great money-making day today at the garage! I've got a few little beauties I'm going to flog to the idiots this morning. Where's my breakfast?'

'It's coming, treasure,' Mrs Wormwood called from the kitchen.

Matilda kept her face bent low over her cornflakes. She didn't dare look up. In the first place she wasn't at all sure what she was going to see. And secondly, if she did see what she thought she was going to see, she wouldn't trust herself to keep a straight face. The son was looking directly ahead out of the window stuffing himself with bread and peanut-butter and strawberry jam.

The father was just moving round to sit at the head of the table when the mother came sweeping out from the kitchen carrying a huge plate piled high with eggs and sausages and bacon and tomatoes. She looked up. She caught sight of her husband. She stopped dead. Then she let out a scream that seemed to lift her right up into the air and she dropped the plate with a crash and a splash on to the floor. Everyone jumped, including Mr Wormwood.

'What the heck's the matter with you, woman?' he shouted. 'Look at the mess you've made on the carpet!'

'Your hair!' the mother was shrieking, pointing a quivering finger at her husband. 'Look at your *hair*! What've you done to your *hair*?'

'What's wrong with my hair, for heaven's sake?' he said.

'Oh my gawd, Dad, what've you done to your hair?' the son shouted.

A splendid noisy scene was building up nicely in the breakfast room.

Matilda said nothing. She simply sat there admiring the wonderful effect of her own handiwork. Mr Wormwood's fine crop of black hair was now a dirty silver, the colour this time of a tightrope-walker's tights that had not been washed for the entire circus season.

'You've . . . you've . . . you've *dyed* it!' shrieked the mother. 'Why did you do it, you fool! It looks absolutely frightful! It looks horrendous! You look like a freak!'

'What the blazes are you all talking about?' the father yelled, putting both hands to his hair. 'I most certainly have not dyed it! What d'you mean I've dyed it? What's happened to it? Or is this some sort of a stupid joke?' His face was turning pale green, the colour of sour apples.

'You must have dyed it, Dad,' the son said. 'It's the same colour as Mum's, only much dirtier-looking.'

'Of course he's dyed it!' the mother cried. 'It can't change colour all by itself! What on earth were you trying to do, make yourself look handsome or something? You look like someone's grandmother gone wrong!'

'Get me a mirror!' the father yelled. 'Don't just stand there shrieking at me! Get me a mirror!'

The mother's handbag lay on a chair at the other end of the table. She opened the bag and got out a powder compact that had a small round mirror on the inside of the lid. She opened the compact and handed it to her husband. He grabbed it and held it before his face and in doing so spilled most of the powder all over the front of his fancy tweed jacket.

'Be *careful*!' shrieked the mother. 'Now look what you've done! That's my best Elizabeth Arden face powder!'

'Oh my gawd!' yelled the father, staring into the little mirror. 'What's happened to me! I look terrible! I look just like *you* gone wrong! I can't go down to the garage and sell cars like this! How did it happen?' He stared round the room, first at the mother, then at the son, then at Matilda. 'How *could* it have happened?' he yelled.

'I imagine, Daddy,' Matilda said quietly, 'that you weren't looking very hard and you simply took Mummy's bottle of hair stuff off the shelf instead of your own.'

'Of *course* that's what happened!' the mother cried. 'Well really, Harry, how stupid can you get? Why didn't you read the label before you started splashing the stuff all over you! Mine's *terribly* strong. I'm only meant to use one tablespoon of it in a whole basin of water and you've gone and put it all over your head neat! It'll probably take all your hair off in the end! Is your scalp beginning to burn, dear?'

'You mean I'm going to lose all my hair?' the husband yelled.

'I think you will,' the mother said. 'Peroxide is a very powerful chemical. It's what they put down the lavatory to disinfect the pan, only they give it another name.'

'What are you saying!' the husband cried. 'I'm not a lavatory pan! I don't want to be disinfected!'

'Even diluted like I use it,' the mother told him, 'it makes a good deal of my hair fall out, so goodness knows what's going to happen to you. I'm surprised it didn't take the whole of the top of your head off!'

'What shall I do?' wailed the father. 'Tell me quick what to do before it starts falling out!'

Matilda said, 'I'd give it a good wash, Dad, if I were you, with soap and water. But you'll have to hurry.'

'Will that change the colour back?' the father asked anxiously.

'Of course it won't, you twit,' the mother said.

'Then what do I do? I can't go around looking like this for ever!'

'You'll have to have it dyed black,' the mother said. 'But wash it first or there won't be any there to dye.'

'Right!' the father shouted, springing into action. 'Get me an appointment with your hairdresser this instant for a hair-dyeing job! Tell them it's an emergency! They've got to boot someone else off their list! I'm going upstairs to wash it now!' With that the man dashed out of the room and Mrs Wormwood, sighing deeply, went to the telephone to call the beauty parlour.

'He does do some pretty silly things now and again, doesn't he, Mummy?' Matilda said.

The mother, dialling the number on the phone, said, 'I'm afraid men are not always quite as clever as they think they are. You will learn that when you get a bit older, my girl.'

But don't do that, do THIS!

★★ TRiCK

Surprise Shampoo

When Roald Dahl
wrote *Matilda*, he claimed that

Oil of Violets Hair Tonic and

PLATINUM BLONDE HAIR-DYE
EXTRA STRONG

could be found in every hairdresser and every
barbershop around the world. Now, they're all gone.
Every single bottle. Don't ask me why. As a writer he
sometimes made things up. And don't panic either.
For different hair effects, try adding these wonderful
ingredients to the nearest shampoo bottle.
Spectacular results are guaranteed.

★ ★ ★

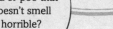
What's the only
kind of poo that
doesn't smell
horrible?
Shampoo!

 Add two teaspoons of **GLITTER** for super-sparkly hair.

 Add a few drops of **FOOD COLOURING** for red or yellow or green or blue or purple hair.

 Or just fill an empty bottle with **CUSTARD**. When applied to hair, this yellow gloop will not make the hair glossy or shiny or sparkly or highlighted. It will not condition dry hair and it will not mean that the owner of long princess hair can swing it round their shoulders in a big curtain of loveliness as if they are starring in a television advert. **It will just look as if a giant bird has pooped on their head.** And how funny would that be?

Augustus Gloop Goes up the Pipe

In which Augustus Gloop learns that drinking from a chocolate river is delicious yet VERY DANGEROUS.

When Mr Wonka turned round and saw what Augustus Gloop was doing, he cried out, 'Oh, no! *Please*, Augustus, *please*! I beg of you not to do that. My chocolate must be untouched by human hands!'

'Augustus!' called out Mrs Gloop. 'Didn't you hear what the man said? Come away from that river at once!'

'This stuff is fabulous!' said Augustus, taking not the slightest notice of his mother or Mr Wonka. 'Gosh, I need a bucket to drink it properly!'

'Augustus,' cried Mr Wonka, hopping up and down and waggling his stick in the air, 'you *must* come away. You are dirtying my chocolate!'

'Augustus!' cried Mrs Gloop.

'Augustus!' cried Mr Gloop.

But Augustus was deaf to everything except the call of his enormous stomach. He was now lying full length on the ground with his head far out over the river, lapping up the chocolate like a dog.

'Augustus!' shouted Mrs Gloop. 'You'll be giving that nasty cold of yours to about a million people all over the country!'

'Be careful, Augustus!' shouted Mr Gloop. 'You're leaning too far out!'

Mr Gloop was absolutely right. For suddenly there was a shriek, and then a splash, and into the river went Augustus Gloop, and in one second he had disappeared under the brown surface.

'Save him!' screamed Mrs Gloop, going white in the face, and waving her umbrella about. 'He'll drown! He can't swim a yard! Save him! Save him!'

'Good heavens, woman,' said Mr Gloop, 'I'm not diving in there! I've got my best suit on!'

Augustus Gloop's face came up again to the surface,

painted brown with chocolate. 'Help! Help! Help!' he yelled. 'Fish me out!'

'Don't just *stand* there!' Mrs Gloop screamed at Mr Gloop. '*Do* something!'

'I *am* doing something!' said Mr Gloop, who was now taking off his jacket and getting ready to dive into the chocolate. But while he was doing this, the wretched boy was being sucked closer and closer towards the mouth of one of the great pipes that was dangling down into the river. Then all at once, the powerful suction took hold of him completely, and he was pulled under the surface and then into the mouth of the pipe.

The crowd on the riverbank waited breathlessly to see where he would come out.

'*There he goes!*' somebody shouted, pointing upwards.

And sure enough, because the pipe was made of glass, Augustus Gloop could be clearly seen shooting up inside it, head first, like a torpedo.

'Help! Murder! Police!' screamed Mrs Gloop. 'Augustus, come back at once! Where are you going?'

'It's a wonder to me,' said Mr Gloop, 'how that pipe is big enough for him to go through it.'

'It *isn't* big enough!' said Charlie Bucket. 'Oh dear, look! He's slowing down!'

'So he is!' said Grandpa Joe.

'He's going to stick!' said Charlie.

'I think he is!' said Grandpa Joe.

'By golly, he *has* stuck!' said Charlie.

'It's his stomach that's done it!' said Mr Gloop.

'He's blocked the whole pipe!' said Grandpa Joe.

'Smash the pipe!' yelled Mrs Gloop, still waving her umbrella. 'Augustus, come out of there at once!'

The watchers below could see the chocolate swishing around the boy in the pipe, and they could see it building up behind him in a solid mass, pushing against the blockage. The pressure was terrific. Something had to give. Something did give, and that something was Augustus. *WHOOF!* Up he shot again like a bullet in the barrel of a gun.

But don't do that, do THIS!

TRICK

The Hot Chocolate That Isn't

Everyone* loves chocolate. So why not take advantage of this fact and play a **FIENDISHLY** naughty trick on someone who simply adores the stuff?

*And if they don't, they clearly need a trip to a chocolate factory to sort them out.

YOU WILL NEED:

What's the best thing to put into a chocolate pie? **Your teeth.**

☆ Two mugs
☆ Four teaspoons of drinking chocolate
☆ Two teaspoons of gravy granules

WHAT YOU DO:

1 Offer to make **hot chocolate** for an adult who loves chocolate.

2 Make a mug of deliciously chocolatey hot chocolate using two teaspoons of drinking chocolate. (Ask an older person who's in on the trick to supervise the hot water or hot milk. You really don't want to spill it on yourself.)

3 Make another mug of deliciously chocolatey hot chocolate using two teaspoons of drinking chocolate **AND two teaspoons of gravy granules**. Stir well.

4 Now take the two drinks into the room where your unsuspecting adult is waiting.

5 Give the mug of choco-gravy to the adult and (this is VERY important) keep the mug of real hot chocolate for yourself.

6 Sip the hot chocolate and say, **'Mmmmmmmmmm...'**

7 Wait for your victim to say, **'BLEURGHHHHHH!'**

Spot the Mischief-maker

Study the clues to identify one of Roald Dahl's STICKIEST, SWEETEST characters ever.

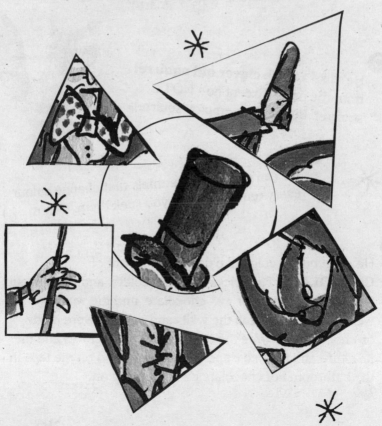

Turn the page for more clues!

1 His voice is high and *flutey*. (Try talking in a high and flutey voice for a whole day. Your family will love it. Seriously.)

What kind of sweet is always late? **A chocolate.**

2 He wears a **black top hat**. He wears a **tail coat** made of beautiful plum-coloured velvet. His **trousers** are bottle green. His **gloves** are pearly grey. (Goodness, how smart!)

3 He's like a quick **clever old squirrel** from the park. (Except he's NOT a squirrel. But he does employ squirrels . . .)

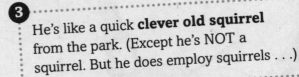

4 He can make rich caramels that change colour every ten seconds as you suck them. (Mmm . . .)

5 He once built a colossal palace entirely out of **CHOCOLATE**. The bricks were chocolate, and the cement holding them together was chocolate, and the windows were chocolate and all the walls and ceilings were made of chocolate, so were the carpets and the pictures and the furniture and the beds; and when you turned on the taps in the bathroom hot chocolate came pouring out.

Who is he?

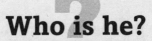

The answer is on page 92.

From The BFG

Capture

*In which Sophie is VERY BRAVE and, with
the help of the BFG, tackles a VERY BIG and
VERY UNFRIENDLY giant.*

Sophie ran up behind the Fleshlumpeater. She was
holding the brooch between her fingers. When she
was right up close to the great naked hairy legs, she
rammed the three-inch-long pin of the brooch as hard
as she could into the Fleshlumpeater's right ankle.
It went deep into the flesh and
stayed there.

   The giant gave
a roar of pain and
jumped high in the
air. He dropped
the soldier and
made a grab for
his ankle.

The BFG, knowing what a coward the Fleshlumpeater was, saw his chance. 'You is bitten by a snake!' he shouted. 'I seed it biting you! It was a frightsome poisnowse viper! It was a dreadly dungerous vindscreen viper!'

'Save our souls!' bellowed the Fleshlumpeater. 'Sound the crumpets! I is bitten by a septicous venomsome vindscreen viper!' He flopped to the ground and sat there howling his head off and clutching his ankle with both hands. His fingers felt the brooch. 'The teeth of the dreadly viper is still sticking into me!' he yelled. 'I is feeling the teeth sticking into my anklet!'

The BFG saw his second chance. 'We must be getting those viper's teeth out at once!' he cried. 'Otherwise you is deader than duck-soup! I is helping you!'

The BFG knelt down beside the Fleshlumpeater. 'You must grab your anklet very tight with both hands!' he ordered. 'That will stop the poisnowse juices from the venomsome viper going up your leg and into your heart!'

The Fleshlumpeater grabbed his ankle with both hands.

'Now close your eyes and grittle your teeth and look up to heaven and say your prayers while I is taking out the teeth of the venomsome viper,' the BFG said.

The terrified Fleshlumpeater did exactly as he was told.

The BFG signalled for some rope. A soldier rushed

it over to him. With both the Fleshlumpeater's hands gripping his ankle, it was a simple matter for the BFG to tie the ankles and hands together with a tight knot.

'I is pulling out the frightsome viper's teeth!' the BFG said as he pulled the knot tight.

'Do it quickly!' shouted the Fleshlumpeater, 'before I is pizzened to death!'

'There we is,' said the BFG, standing up. 'You can look now.'

When the Fleshlumpeater saw that he was trussed up like a turkey, he gave a yell so loud that the heavens trembled. He rolled and he wriggled, he fought and he figgled, he squirmed and he squiggled. But there was not a thing he could do.

'Well done you!' Sophie cried.

'Well done *you*!' said the BFG, smiling down at the little girl. 'You is saving all of our lives!'

'Will you please get that brooch back for me,' Sophie said. 'It belongs to the Queen.'

But don't do that, do THIS!

Four Ways To Trick A Giant

Unless you live in a land of thick forests and rushing rivers and hills as bare as concrete and ground that is flat and pale yellow, with great lumps of blue rock scattered around and dead trees standing around like skeletons – which is the land where the **BFG** lives – then you are unlikely to meet a real live **giant**. So the next biggest thing is a really tall grown-up. Trick one of those instead!

1 **Take the batteries out of the TV remote control.** Hide them. Replace the remote control. Now it will be more entertaining watching the grown-up trying to make the TV work than the TV itself! (For an even better trick, secretly replace the batteries and then tell the grown-up that they must have been doing it wrong, because – look! – the remote control is working **PERFECTLY**.)

2 **Stuff newspaper inside shoes.** Make sure it's right down at the toes so the grown-up doesn't see it before they put their feet in. Fill **ALL** shoes and boots, even ones that the grown-up hardly ever wears, for fun **ALL THROUGH THE YEAR.** How they'll laugh!

3 **Change the time on the clocks.** All of the clocks. Get up really early one morning and move them an hour forward. Then **EVERYONE** will be an hour early for work and school. Except you. You can have a lie-in. **Bwa-ha-haaa!**

4 **Press the volume button on the TV remote control** to the loudest it will go when it is turned off. The next person who turns on the TV will have the **FRIGHT OF HIS OR HER LIFE!**

When is a magician in a car not a magician in a car? **When he turns into a driveway.**

Spot the Mischief-maker

**Can you work out which
Roald Dahl character this is?**

1 He is clever. How clever? Probably cleverer than all of your teachers at school and **Newton** and **Einstein** and **Professor Stephen Hawking** put together. THAT clever. And then some.

What do you say to a magician with white rabbits in his ears? **Anything you like – he can't hear you.**

2 He has a long handsome face.

3 He has had the finest tail for miles around, until . . . Well, THAT would be giving the game away.

4 He doesn't like farmers, especially not **Farmers Boggis**, **Farmer Bunce** and **Farmer Bean**. And you wouldn't either if you knew them.

5 He is **FANTASTIC**. (Have you got it yet? Have you? HAVE YOU? Because this is officially the Biggest Clue Ever.)

Who is he?

The answer is on page 92.

The Marvellous Plan

In which George decides to make his very own magic medicine to treat his horrid grandma.

George sat himself down at the table in the kitchen. He was shaking a little. Oh, how he hated Grandma! He really *hated* that horrid old witchy woman. And all of a sudden he had a tremendous urge to *do something* about her. Something *whopping*. Something *absolutely terrific*. A *real shocker*. A sort of explosion. He wanted to blow away the witchy smell that hung about her in the next room. He may have been only eight years old but he was a brave little boy. He was ready to take this old woman on.

'I'm not going to be frightened by *her*,' he said softly to himself. But he *was* frightened. And that's why he wanted suddenly to explode her away.

Well . . . not quite away. But he did want to shake the old woman up a bit.

Very well, then.What should it be, this whopping terrific exploding shocker for Grandma?

He would have liked to put a firework banger under her chair but he didn't have one.

He would have liked to put a long green snake down the back of her dress but he didn't have a long green snake.

He would have liked to put six big black rats in the room with her and lock the door but he didn't have six big black rats.

As George sat there pondering this interesting problem, his eye fell upon the bottle of Grandma's brown medicine standing on the sideboard. Rotten stuff it seemed to be. Four times a day a large spoonful of it was shovelled into her mouth and it didn't do her the slightest bit of good. She was always just as horrid after she'd had it as she'd been before.

The whole point of medicine, surely, was to make a person better. If it didn't do that, then it was quite useless.

So-ho! thought George suddenly. *Ah-ha! Hohum!* I know exactly what I'll do. I shall make her a *new* medicine, one that is so strong and so fierce and so fantastic it will either cure her completely or blow off the top of her head. I'll make her a *magic medicine*, a medicine no doctor in the world has ever made before.

George looked at the kitchen clock. It said five past ten. There was nearly an hour left before Grandma's next dose was due at eleven.

'Here we go, then!' cried George, jumping up from the table. 'A magic medicine it shall be!'

'So give me a bug and a jumping flea,
Give me two snails and lizards three,
And a slimy squiggler from the sea,
And the poisonous sting of a bumblebee,
And the juice from the fruit of the ju-jube
    tree,
And the powdered bone of a wombat's
    knee.
And one hundred other things as well
Each with a rather nasty smell.

I'll stir them up, I'll boil them long,
A mixture tough, a mixture strong.
And then, heigh-ho, and down it goes,
A nice big spoonful (hold your nose)
Just gulp it down and have no fear.
"How do you like it, Granny dear?"
Will she go pop? Will she explode?
Will she go flying down the road?
Will she go poof in a puff of smoke?
Start fizzing like a can of Coke?
Who knows? Not I. Let's wait and see.
(I'm glad it's neither you nor me.)
Oh Grandma, if you only knew
What I have got in store for you!'

But don't do that, do THIS!

★★ TRICK

A Recipe for Chocolate and Brussels Sprout Pie

It's a well-known fact that grown-ups adore eating vegetables nearly as much as they adore making younger people eat vegetables. So they are bound to LOVE this delightful pie. Why not rustle one up at the weekend, feed it to the grown-ups of your choice and THEN get them to guess what's in it?

PS If they make lots of weird noises like **BLEURGH** and **EEUCH**, tell them that it's good for them and not to whinge. Just like they tell you.

YOU WILL NEED:

☆ One spoonful of butter or margarine or posh spread made from olives

☆ One pie dish

☆ One rolling pin

☆ One packet of puff pastry

☆ One bag of Brussels sprouts

☆ One bar of very dark chocolate

☆ One egg

☆ One oven

☆ One group of grown-ups, preferably the healthy sort

OPTIONAL INGREDIENTS:
Cabbage, Marmite, chocolate sprinkles, syrup, baked beans, puréed pumpkin, jam, tinned carrots and sardines. Mmm.

WHAT YOU DO:

1 **Rub** the butter, margarine or posh spread made from olives into your pie dish.

2 **Roll out two circles of pastry.** Put one of them into your pie dish.

3 Put the **Brussels sprouts** into the pie dish.

4 Break the **chocolate** up into squares and put that in too.

5 Add as many of the optional ingredients as you like.

6 Place the other circle of pastry on top of the pie dish and **seal the pastry round the edges** by pinching them together.

7 **Paint the top of the pie** with beaten egg, just to make it look super appetizing when it's cooked.

8 **Ask an adult to help you pop it in the oven.** Bake for 45 minutes to an hour at 190° C or Gas Mark 5.

From Boy

Goat's Tobacco

*In which Roald Dahl swaps tobacco for
something EVEN SMELLIER.*

One day, we all went in our little motor-boat to an
island we had never been to before, and for once the
ancient half-sister and the manly lover decided to
come with us. We chose this particular island because
we saw some goats on it. They were climbing about
on the rocks and we thought it would be fun to go and
visit them. But when we landed, we found that the
goats were totally wild and we couldn't get near them.
So we gave up trying to make friends with them and
simply sat around on the smooth rocks in our bathing
costumes, enjoying the lovely sun.

The manly lover was filling his pipe. I happened
to be watching him as he very carefully packed the

tobacco into the bowl from a yellow oilskin pouch. He had just finished doing this and was about to light up when the ancient half-sister called on him to come swimming. So he put down the pipe and off he went.

I stared at the pipe that was lying there on the rocks. About twelve inches away from it, I saw a little heap of dried goat's droppings, each one small and round like a pale brown berry, and at that point, an interesting idea began to sprout in my mind. I picked up the pipe and knocked all the tobacco out of it. I then took the goat's droppings and teased them with my fingers until they were nicely shredded. Very gently I poured these shredded droppings into the bowl of the pipe, packing them down with my thumb just as the manly lover always did it. When that was done, I placed a thin layer of real tobacco over the top. The entire family was watching me as I did this. Nobody said a word, but I could sense a glow of approval all round. I replaced the pipe on the rock, and all of us sat back to await the return of the victim. The whole lot of us were in this together now, even my mother. I had drawn them into the plot simply by letting them see what I was doing. It was a silent, rather dangerous family conspiracy.

Back came the manly lover, dripping wet from the sea, chest out, strong and virile, healthy and sunburnt. 'Great swim!' he announced to the world. 'Splendid water! Terrific stuff!' He towelled himself vigorously, making the muscles of his biceps ripple, then he sat down on the rocks and reached for his pipe.

Nine pairs of eyes watched him intently. Nobody giggled to give the game away. We were trembling with anticipation, and a good deal of the suspense was caused by the fact that none of us knew just what was going to happen.

The manly lover put the pipe between his strong white teeth and struck a match. He held the flame over the bowl and sucked. The tobacco ignited and glowed, and the lover's head was enveloped in clouds of blue smoke. 'Ah-h-h,' he said, blowing smoke through his nostrils. 'There's nothing like a good pipe after a bracing swim.'

Still we waited. We could hardly bear the suspense. The sister who was seven couldn't bear it at all. 'What *sort* of tobacco do you put in that thing?' she asked with superb innocence.

'Navy Cut,' the male lover answered. 'Player's Navy Cut. It's the best there is. These Norwegians use all sorts of disgusting scented tobaccos, but I wouldn't touch them.'

'I didn't know they had different tastes,' the small sister went on.

'Of course they do,' the manly lover said. 'All tobaccos are different to the discriminating pipe-smoker. Navy Cut is clean and unadulterated. It's a man's smoke.' The man seemed to go out of his way to use long words like discriminating and unadulterated. We hadn't the foggiest what they meant.

The ancient half-sister, fresh from her swim and now clothed in a towel bathrobe, came and sat herself

close to her manly lover. Then the two of them started giving each other those silly little glances and soppy smiles that made us all feel sick. They were far too occupied with one another to notice the awful tension that had settled over our group. They didn't even notice that every face in the crowd was turned towards them. They had sunk once again into their lovers' world where little children did not exist.

The sea was calm, the sun was shining and it was a beautiful day.

Then all of a sudden, the manly lover let out a piercing scream and his whole body shot about four feet into the air. His pipe flew out of his mouth and went clattering over the rocks, and the second scream he gave was so shrill and loud that all the seagulls on the island rose up in alarm. His features were twisted like those of a person undergoing severe torture, and his skin had turned the colour of snow. He began spluttering and choking and spewing and hawking and acting generally like a man with some serious internal injury. He was completely speechless.

We stared at him, enthralled.

The ancient half-sister, who must have thought she was about to lose her future husband for ever, was pawing at him and thumping him on the back and crying, 'Darling! Darling! What's happening to you? Where does it hurt? Get the boat! Start the engine! We must rush him to a hospital quickly!' She seemed to have forgotten that there wasn't a hospital within fifty miles.

'I've been poisoned!' spluttered the manly lover. 'It's got into my lungs! It's in my chest! My chest is on fire! My stomach's going up in flames!'

'Help me get him into the boat! Quick!' cried the ancient half-sister, gripping him under the armpits. 'Don't just sit there staring! Come and help!'

'No, no, no!' cried the now not-so-manly lover. 'Leave me alone! I need air! Give me air!' He lay back and breathed in deep draughts of splendid Norwegian ocean air, and in another minute or so, he was sitting up again and was on the way to recovery.

'What in the world came over you?' asked the ancient half-sister, clasping his hands tenderly in hers.

'I can't imagine,' he murmured. 'I simply can't imagine.' His face was as still and white as virgin snow and his hands were trembling. 'There must be a reason for it,' he added. 'There's got to be a reason.'

'I know the reason!' shouted the seven-year-old sister, screaming with laughter. 'I know what it was!'

'What was it?' snapped the ancient one. 'What have you been up to? Tell me at once!'

'It's his pipe!' shouted the small sister, still convulsed with laughter.

'What's wrong with my pipe?' said the manly lover.

'You've been smoking goat's tobacco!' cried the small sister.

It took a few moments for the full meaning of these words to dawn upon the two lovers, but when it did, and when the terrible anger began to show itself on the manly lover's face, and when he started to rise slowly and menacingly to his feet, we all sprang up and ran for our lives and jumped off the rocks into the deep water.

But don't do that, do THIS!

★★ TRiCK

Super Poop

You don't have to grub about collecting **goat's poop** like Roald Dahl did. (Well, you can if you want to, but make sure you wash your hands afterwards.) It's much more fun using . . .

FAKE POOP

Chocolate-covered raisins are perfect. Scatter these around the house and tell everyone they are mouse or squirrel or small donkey droppings. And if you really want to shock your audience pick one up, pop it in your mouth and declare it to be **'DELICIOUS'**.*

* Stand by to catch any great-aunts. This is the sort of thing that might make them faint with horror.

Spot the Mischief-maker

Who is THIS loathsome Roald Dahl character?

What flavour squash do Vermicious Knids like to drink? **Lemon and slime.**

1 She has horrible laughter.

Hahahahaaaaaaargh.

2 She had quite a nice face when she was young . . .

3 . . . but now she is fearfully **ugly**.

4 She carries a **walking stick**, not to help her to walk but so that she can hit things with it, like **dogs** and **cats** and small **children**.

5 She has a glass eye.

Who is she?

The answer is on page 92.

From Danny the Champion of the World

Into the Wood

In which Danny and his father risk life, limb and bottom to poach pheasants from right under the nose of the gamekeeper.

We crouched close to the ground, watching the keeper. He was a smallish man with a cap on his head and a big double-barrelled shotgun under his arm. He never moved. He was like a little post standing there.

'Should we go?' I whispered.

The keeper's face was shadowed by the peak of his cap, but it seemed to me he was looking straight at us.

'Should we go, Dad?'

'Hush,' my father said.

Slowly, never taking his eyes from the keeper, he reached into his pocket and brought out a single raisin. He placed it in the palm of his right hand, and then quickly with a little flick of the wrist he threw the raisin high into the air. I watched it as it went sailing over the bushes and I saw it land within a yard of two hen birds standing beside an old tree-stump. Both birds turned their heads sharply at the drop of the raisin. Then one of them hopped over and made a quick peck at the ground and that must have been it.

I looked at the keeper. He hadn't moved.

I could feel a trickle of cold sweat running down one side of my forehead and across my cheek. I didn't dare lift a hand to wipe it away.

My father threw a second raisin into the clearing . . . then a third . . . and a fourth . . . and a fifth.

It takes guts to do that, I thought. Terrific guts. If I'd been alone I would never have stayed there for one second. But my father was in a sort of poacher's trance. For him, this was it. This was the moment of danger, the biggest thrill of all.

He kept on throwing the raisins into the clearing, swiftly, silently, one at a time. Flick went his wrist, and up went the raisin, high over the bushes, to land among the pheasants.

Then all at once, I saw the keeper turn away his head to inspect the wood behind him.

My father saw it too. Quick as a flash, he pulled the bag of raisins out of his pocket and tipped the whole lot into the palm of his right hand.

'Dad!' I whispered. 'Don't!'

But with a great sweep of the arm he flung the entire handful way over the bushes into the clearing.

They fell with a soft little patter, like raindrops on dry leaves, and every single pheasant in the place must have heard them fall. There was a flurry of wings and a rush to find the treasure.

The keeper's head flicked round as though there were a spring inside his neck. The birds were all pecking away madly at the raisins. The keeper took two quick paces forward, and for a moment I thought he was going in to investigate. But then he stopped, and his face came up and his eyes began travelling slowly round the edge of the clearing.

'Lie down flat!' my father whispered. 'Stay there! Don't move an inch!'

I flattened my body against the ground and pressed one side of my face into the brown leaves. The soil below the leaves had a queer pungent smell, like beer. Out of one eye, I saw my father raise his head just a tiny bit to watch the keeper. He kept watching him.

'Don't you *love* this?' he whispered to me.

I didn't dare answer him.

We lay there for what seemed like a hundred years.

At last I heard my father whisper, 'Panic's over. Follow me, Danny. But be extra careful, he's still

there. And *keep down low all the time.*'

He started crawling away quickly on his hands and knees. I went after him. I kept thinking of the keeper who was somewhere behind us. I was very conscious of that keeper, and I was also very conscious of my own backside, and how it was sticking up in the air for all to see. I could understand now why 'poacher's bottom' was a fairly common complaint in this business.

We went along on our hands and knees for about a hundred yards.

'Now run!' my father said.

We got to our feet and ran, and a few minutes later we came out through the hedge into the lovely open safety of the cart-track.

'It went marvellously!' my father said, breathing heavily. 'Didn't it go absolutely marvellously?' His face was scarlet and glowing with triumph.

'Did the keeper see us?' I asked.

'Not on your life!' he said. 'And in a few minutes the sun will be going down and the birds will all be flying up to roost and that keeper will be sloping off home to his supper. Then all we've got to do is go back in again and help ourselves. We'll be picking them up off the ground like pebbles!'

He sat down on the grassy bank below the hedge. I sat down close to him. He put an arm round my shoulders and gave me a hug. 'You did well, Danny,' he said. 'I'm right proud of you.'

But don't do that, do THIS!

☆ TRiCK

Poach an Egg, Not a Pheasant

Poach an egg. (Ask an adult to help with the hot-water bit.) It's easier than poaching pheasants – and a lot more legal. Better still, boil an egg for **a REALLY good yolk**. (Ha ha! Ahem. Sorry – joke, not yolk.) Pop the hard-boiled egg back in the egg box when you're done. Then be ready to laugh **REALLY LOUDLY** when someone tries to crack it.

The Recipe

*In which The Grand High Witch describes the spell that
will turn children into mice at PRECISELY nine o'clock
the next morning, just in time for school.*

'Attention again!' The Grand High Witch was shouting.
'I vill now give to you the rrrecipe for concocting
Formula 86 Delayed Action Mouse-Maker! Get out
pencils and paper.'

Handbags were opened all over the room and
notebooks were fished out.

'Give us the recipe, O Brainy One!' cried the audience impatiently. 'Tell us the secret.'

'First,' said The Grand High Witch, 'I had to find something that vould cause the children to become very small very qvickly.'

'And what was that?' cried the audience.

'That part vos simple,' said The Grand High Witch. 'All you have to do if you are vishing to make a child very small is to look at him through the wrrrong end of a telescope.'

'She's a wonder!' cried the audience. 'Who else would have thought of a thing like that?'

'So you take the wrrrong end of a telescope,' continued The Grand High Witch, 'and you boil it until it gets soft.'

'How long does that take?' they asked her.

'Tventy-vun hours of boiling,' answered The Grand High Witch. 'And vhile this is going on, you take exactly forty-five brrrown mice and you chop off their tails vith a carving-knife and you fry the tails in hair-oil until they are nice and crrrisp.'

'What do we do with all those mice who have had their tails chopped off?' asked the audience.

'You simmer them in frog-juice for vun hour,' came the answer. 'But listen to me. So far I have only given you the easy part of the rrrecipe. The rrreally difficult problem is to put in something that vill have a genuine delayed action rrree-sult, something that can be eaten by children on a certain day but vhich vill not start vurrrking on them until nine o'clock the next morning vhen they arrive at school.'

'What did you come up with, O Brainy One?' they called out. 'Tell us the great secret!'

'The secret,' announced The Grand High Witch triumphantly, 'is an *alarm-clock*!'

'An alarm-clock!' they cried. 'It's a stroke of genius!'

'Of course it is,' said The Grand High Witch.

'You can set a tventy-four-hour alarm-clock today and at exactly nine o'clock tomorrow it vill go off.'

'But we will need five million alarm-clocks!' cried the audience. 'We will need one for each child!'

'Idiots!' shouted The Grand High Witch. 'If you are vonting a steak, you do not cook the whole cow! It is the same vith alarm-clocks. Vun clock vill make enough for a thousand children. Here is vhat you do. You set your alarm-clock to go off at nine o'clock tomorrow morning.

Then you rrroast it in the oven until it is crrrisp and tender. Are you wrrriting this down?'

'We are, Your Grandness, we are!' they cried.

'Next,' said The Grand High Witch, 'you take your boiled telescope and your frrried mouse-tails and your cooked mice and your rrroasted alarm-clock and all together you put them into the mixer. Then you mix

them at full speed. This vill give you a nice thick paste. Vhile the mixer is still mixing you must add to it the yolk of vun grrruntle's egg.'

'A gruntle's egg!' cried the audience. 'We shall do that!'

 Underneath all the clamour that was going on I heard one witch in the back row saying to her neighbour, 'I'm getting a bit old to go bird's nesting. Those ruddy gruntles always nest very high up.'

'So you mix in the egg,' The Grand High Witch went on, 'and vun after the other you also mix in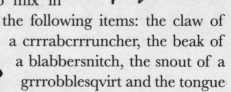

 the following items: the claw of a crrrabcrrruncher, the beak of a blabbersnitch, the snout of a grrrobblesqvirt and the tongue

of a catsprrringer. I trust you are not having any trrrouble finding those.'

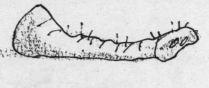

'None at all!' they cried out. 'We will spear the blabbersnitch and trap the crabcruncher and shoot the grobblesquirt and catch the catspringer in his burrow!'

'Excellent!' said The Grand High Witch. 'Vhen you have mixed everything together in the mixer, you vill have a most marvellous-looking grrreen liqvid. Put vun drop, just vun titchy droplet, of this liqvid into a chocolate or a sveet, and *at nine o'clock the next morning* the child who ate it vill turn into a mouse in twenty-six seconds! But vun vurd of vorning. Never increase the dose. Never put more than vun drrrop into each sveet or chocolate. And never give more than vun sweet or chocolate to each child. An overdose of Delayed Action Mouse-Maker vill mess up the timing of the alarm-clock and cause the child to turn into a mouse too early. A large overdose might even have an instant effect, and you vouldn't vont that, vould you? You vouldn't vont the children turning into mice rrright there in your svect-shops. That vould give the game away. So be very carrreful! Do not overdose!'

But don't do that, do THIS!

TRICK

The Great Mouse Trick

THE GRAND HIGH WITCH'S
Formula 86 Delayed Action Mouse-Maker

is probably not a spell you want to cast on your friends. (Not if you ever want them to speak – or even **SQUEAK** – to you again.) Instead, try this harmless yet **HILARIOUS** trick. All you need to do is stick a tiny piece of sticky tape over the optical sensor underneath a computer mouse and, as if by magic, it won't work.

PS This would usually be labelled a one-star trick. The extra star is awarded because of the high risk of sending grown-ups **STARK STARING BONKERS** when they discover that their computer doesn't work properly. If your particular adult displays danger signs – **turns beetroot, starts growling, stamps feet, shouts a lot** – suggest that they turn the computer off and on again while you secretly remove the sticky tape . . . and then declare yourself a **computer genius**!

Boggis's Chicken House

Number One

In which Mr Fox and his four children bravely tunnel to Chicken House Number One to find their dinner.

'This time we must go in a very special direction,' said Mr Fox, pointing sideways and downward.

So he and his four children started to dig once again. The work went much more slowly now. Yet they kept at it with great courage, and little by little the tunnel began to grow.

'Dad, I wish you would tell us *where* we are going,' said one of the children.

'I dare not do that,' said Mr Fox, 'because this place I am *hoping* to get to is so *marvellous* that if I described it to you now you would go crazy with excitement. And then, if we failed to get there (which is very possible), you would die of disappointment. I don't want to raise your hopes too much, my darlings.'

For a long long time they kept on digging. For how long they did not know, because there were no days and no nights down there in the murky tunnel. But at last Mr Fox gave the order to stop. 'I think,' he said, 'we had better take a peep upstairs now and see where we are. I know where I *want* to be, but I can't possibly be sure we're anywhere near it.'

Slowly, wearily, the foxes began to slope the tunnel up towards the surface. Up and up it went . . . until suddenly they came to something hard above their heads and they couldn't go up any further. Mr Fox reached up to examine this hard thing. 'It's wood!' he whispered. 'Wooden planks!'

'What does that mean, Dad?'

'It means, unless I am very much mistaken, that we are right underneath somebody's house,' whispered Mr Fox. 'Be very quiet now while I take a peek.'

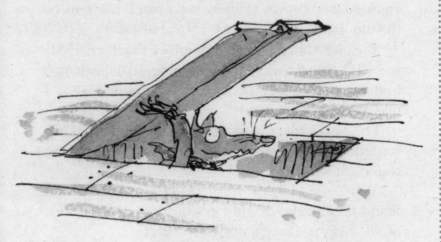

Carefully, Mr Fox began pushing up one of the floorboards. The board creaked most terribly and they all ducked down, waiting for something awful to happen. Nothing did. So Mr Fox pushed up a second board. And then, very very cautiously, he poked his head up through the gap. He let out a shriek of excitement.

'*I've done it!*' he yelled. 'I've done it *first time*! *I've done it! I've done it!*' He pulled himself up through the gap in the floor and started prancing and dancing with joy. 'Come on up!' he sang out. 'Come up and see where you are, my darlings! What a sight for a hungry fox! Hallelujah! Hooray! Hooray!'

The four Small Foxes scrambled up out of the tunnel and what a fantastic sight it was that now met their eyes! They were in a huge shed and the whole place was teeming with chickens. There were white chickens and brown chickens and black chickens by the thousand!

'Boggis's Chicken House Number One!' cried Mr Fox. 'It's exactly what I was aiming at! I hit it slap in the middle! First time! Isn't that fantastic! *And*, if I may say so, rather clever!'

The Small Foxes went wild with excitement. They started running around in all directions, chasing the stupid chickens.

'Wait!' ordered Mr Fox. 'Don't lose your heads! Stand back! Calm down! Let's do this properly! First of all, everyone have a drink of water!'

They all ran over to the chickens' drinking-trough and lapped up the lovely cool water. Then Mr Fox chose three of the plumpest hens, and with a clever flick of his jaws he killed them instantly.

'Back to the tunnel!' he ordered. 'Come on! No fooling around! The quicker you move, the quicker you shall have something to eat!'

One after another, they climbed down through

the hole in the floor and soon they were all standing once again in the dark tunnel. Mr Fox reached up and pulled the floorboards back into place. He did this with great care. He did it so that no one could tell they had ever been moved.

But don't do that, do THIS!

★★★ TRICK

How to Steal a Prehistoric Creature

If you're reading this book, there's a big chance you're not a fox. So there's really no need for you to steal a chicken. (Besides, you can buy them in all good supermarkets.) Instead, why not go for something **HYSTERICALLY historical**, like . . . a **DODO**!

YOU WILL NEED:

- ☆ One time machine
- ☆ One sherry trifle
- ☆ One net

What do you call a swarm of monster bees? **Zombees.**

WHAT YOU DO:

1 **Construct a time machine.**
(At the time of writing, there
were no instructions available for
how to make a time machine, but we
are reasonably confident that you could
knock one up using a **large glass box** –
rather like the one from *Charlie and the Great Glass
Elevator* – **a large ball of string, a gearstick from
a 1979 Mini 1275GT, a Mars bar, a crystal ball
and a jetpack**.)

2 **Make a sherry trifle.**

3 **Set the time machine to any date before 1662**,
which is when the dodo was last spotted before
becoming extinct FOREVER.

4 **Travel through time.**

5 **Land.**

6 Disembark the time machine and **locate your dodo**.
(Don't worry about it flying away. It can't.)

7 Lure the dodo into your time machine with the
sherry trifle. (No records exist confirming that
dodos liked sherry trifle, but WHO DOESN'T?)

8 Travel back through time to **NOW**.

9 **Take the dodo to a top zoologist** and become
famous for bringing the world's most fabulous
flightless bird back from the dead.

10 There – that's more exciting than stealing
a chicken, isn't it?

Spot the Mischief-maker

Who is this mischievous chap from one of Roald Dahl's marvellous storybooks?

What's a rabbit's favourite music? **Hip hop.**

1 His father is a **farmer**.

2 He likes **chocolate**.

3 He doesn't like **cabbage**.

4 He's a **brave** little boy.

5 He doesn't have a **brother** or a **sister**.

Who is he?

The answer is on page 92.

From Revolting Rhymes

Little Red Riding Hood and the Wolf

In which Roald Dahl twists and turns and warps and bends the well-known story of Little Red Riding Hood into something QUITE different.

As soon as Wolf began to feel
That he would like a decent meal,
He went and knocked on Grandma's door.
When Grandma opened it, she saw
The sharp white teeth, the horrid grin,
And Wolfie said, 'May I come in?'
Poor Grandmamma was terrified,
'He's going to eat me up,' she cried.
And she was absolutely right.
He ate her up in one big bite.
But Grandmamma was small and tough,
And Wolfie wailed, 'That's not enough!
'I haven't yet begun to feel

'That I have had a decent meal!'
He ran around the kitchen yelping,
'I've *got* to have another helping!'

Then added with a frightful leer,
'I'm therefore going to wait right here
'Till Little Miss Red Riding Hood
'Comes home from walking in the wood.'
He quickly put on Grandma's clothes.
(Of course he hadn't eaten those.)
He dressed himself in coat and hat.

He put on shoes and after that
He even brushed and curled his hair,
Then sat himself in Grandma's chair.
In came the little girl in red.
She stopped. She stared. And then she said,

'*What great big ears you have, Grandma.*'
'*All the better to hear you with,*' the Wolf replied.
'*What great big eyes you have, Grandma,*'
    said Little Red Riding Hood.
'*All the better to see you with,*' the Wolf replied.

He sat there watching her and smiled.
He thought, I'm going to eat this child.
Compared with her old Grandmamma
She's going to taste like caviare.

Then Little Red Riding Hood said, '*But Grandma,
what a lovely great big furry coat you have on.*'

'That's wrong!' cried Wolf. 'Have you forgot
'To tell me what BIG TEETH I've got?
'Ah well, no matter what you say,
'I'm going to eat you anyway.'
The small girl smiles. One eyelid flickers.
She whips a pistol from her knickers.
She aims it at the creature's head
And *bang bang bang*, she shoots him dead.
A few weeks later, in the wood,
I came across Miss Riding Hood.
But what a change! No cloak of red,
No silly hood upon her head.
She said, 'Hello, and do please note
'My lovely furry WOLFSKIN COAT.'

From The Twits

The Glass Eye

*In which Mrs Twit shows Mr Twit that
she has eyes EVERYWHERE.*

You can play a lot of tricks with a glass eye because
you can take it out and pop it back in again any time
you like. You can bet your life Mrs Twit knew all the
tricks.

One morning she took out her glass eye and dropped it into Mr Twit's mug of beer when he wasn't looking.

Mr Twit sat there drinking the beer slowly. The froth made a white ring on the hairs around his mouth. He wiped the white froth on to his sleeve and wiped his sleeve on his trousers.

'You're plotting something,' Mrs Twit said, keeping her back turned so he wouldn't see that she had taken out her glass eye. 'Whenever you go all quiet like that I know very well you're plotting something.'

Mrs Twit was right. Mr Twit was plotting away like mad. He was trying to think up a really nasty trick he could play on his wife that day.

'You'd better be careful,' Mrs Twit said, 'because when I see you starting to plot, I watch you like a wombat.'

'Oh, do shut up, you old hag,' Mr Twit said. He went on drinking his beer, and his evil mind kept working away on the latest horrid trick he was going to play on the old woman.

Suddenly, as Mr Twit tipped the last drop of beer down his throat, he caught sight of Mrs Twit's awful glass eye staring up at him from the bottom of the mug. It made him jump.

'I told you I was watching you,' cackled Mrs Twit. 'I've got eyes everywhere so you'd better be careful.'

But don't do that, do THIS!

TRiCK

The Joke Eye

You don't need a glass eye to play the same trick as Mrs Twit. Oh no. Here's a much tastier alternative.

YOU WILL NEED:
- ☆ One lychee (a fancy white fruit that looks VERY like an eyeball and tastes DELICIOUS)
- ☆ One green olive
- ☆ One raisin
- ☆ One teaspoon
- ☆ One cocktail stick or toothpick

What do you call an alien with three eyes? **An aliiien.**

WHAT YOU DO:

1 Using your teaspoon, **hollow out the lychee** until you have made an **olive-sized hole**.

2 Put the olive into the hole.

3 Now use your cocktail stick or toothpick to make a **raisin-sized hole in the olive**.

4 Put the raisin into the hole.

5 *Voilà*! You've made a **joke eye**! The lychee is the white of the eye, the olive the iris and the raisin the pupil.

6 Now all you have to do is pop the joke eye in your unsuspecting victim's drink and wait for them to

SCREEEEEEEEEEEAM!

Something Nasty in the Lifts

In which Charlie Bucket and Mr and Mrs Bucket and Grandpa Jo and Grandma Josephine and Grandpa George and Grandma Georgina and Willy Wonka meet ONE OF THE SCARIEST ALIENS IN THE UNIVERSE. Yikes!

It looked more than anything like an enormous egg balanced on its pointed end. It was as tall as a big boy and wider than the fattest man. The greenish-brown skin had a shiny wettish appearance and there were wrinkles in it. About three-quarters of the way up, in the widest part, there were two large round eyes as big as tea-cups. The eyes were white, but each had a brilliant red pupil in the centre. The red pupils were resting on Mr Wonka. But now they began travelling slowly across to Charlie and Grandpa Joe and the others by the bed, settling upon them and gazing at them with a cold malevolent stare. The eyes were everything. There were no other features, no nose or mouth or ears, but the entire egg-shaped body was itself moving very very slightly, pulsing and bulging gently here and there as though the skin were filled with some thick fluid.

At this point, Charlie suddenly noticed that the next lift was coming down. The indicator numbers above the door were flashing . . . 6 . . . 5 . . . 4 . . . 3 . . . 2 . . . 1 . . . L (for lobby). There was a slight pause. The door slid open and there, inside the second lift, was another enormous slimy wrinkled greenish-brown egg with eyes!

Now the numbers were flashing above all three of the remaining lifts. Down they came . . . down . . . down . . . down . . . And soon, at precisely the same time, they reached the lobby floor and the doors slid open . . . five open doors now . . . one creature in each . . . five in all . . . and five pairs of eyes with brilliant red centres all watching Mr Wonka and watching Charlie and Grandpa Joe and the others.

There were slight differences in size and shape between the five, but all had the same greenish-brown wrinkled skin and the skin was rippling and pulsing.

For about thirty seconds nothing happened. Nobody stirred, nobody made a sound. The silence was terrible. So was the suspense. Charlie was so frightened he felt himself shrinking inside his skin. Then he saw the creature in the left-hand lift suddenly starting to change shape! Its body was slowly becoming longer and longer, and thinner and thinner, going up and up towards the roof of the lift, not straight up, but curving a little to the left, making a snake-like curve that was curiously graceful, up to the left and then curling over the top to the right and coming down again in a half-circle . . . and then the bottom end began to grow out as well, like a tail . . . creeping along the floor . . . creeping along the floor to the left . . . until at last the creature, which had originally looked like a huge egg, now looked like a long curvy serpent standing up on its tail.

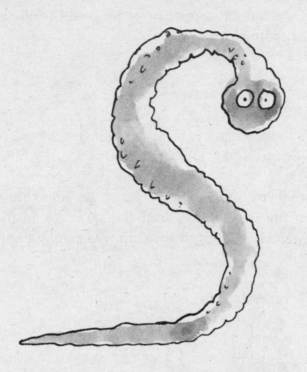

Then the one in the next lift began stretching itself in much the same way, and what a weird and oozy thing it was to watch! It was twisting itself into a shape that was a bit different from the first, balancing itself almost but not quite on the tip of its tail.

Then the three remaining creatures began stretching themselves all at the same time, each one elongating itself slowly upward, growing taller and taller, thinner and thinner, curving and twisting, stretching and stretching, curling and bending, balancing either on the tail or the head or both, and turned sideways now so that only one eye was visible.

When they had all stopped stretching and bending, this was how they finished up:

'*Scram!*' shouted Mr Wonka. 'Get out quick!'

People have never moved faster than Grandpa Joe and Charlie and Mr and Mrs Bucket at that moment. They all got behind the bed and started pushing like crazy. Mr Wonka ran in front of them shouting 'Scram! Scram! Scram!' and in ten seconds flat all of them were out of the lobby and back inside the Great Glass Elevator. Frantically, Mr Wonka began undoing bolts and pressing buttons. The door of the Great Glass Elevator snapped shut and the whole thing leaped sideways. They were away! And of course all of them, including the three old ones in the bed, floated up again into the air.

But don't do that, do THIS!

★★☆ TRiCK

The Daring Plan to Trap a Vermicious Knid

By now, you must be fairly accomplished at carrying out **plots**, **plans**, **japes** and **jokes**, but this is a plan to test even the most experienced mischief-maker. You're going to trap a **Vermicious Knid**. Fail and you'll be, um . . . Well, let's not go into that here. Succeed and you'll be made a knight or a dame or, at the very least, a very important person with a certificate to prove it **RIGHT AWAY**. (Probably.)

YOU WILL NEED:

☆ One spacesuit and helmet (help the environment by re-using the spacesuit and helmet from **The Sticky Rocket** on page 40)

☆ One space rocket

☆ One oval gilt-edged mirror and superglue

☆ One butterfly net

☆ One good book (*Charlie and the Great Glass Elevator* is perfect)

☆ One MP3 player (with speakers) loaded with some beautiful love songs

WHAT YOU DO:

Wearing the **spacesuit and helmet**, climb on-board the rocket and blast off in the direction of **deep space**.

Settle down with your good book. (Luckily, the time it will take you to read *Charlie and the Great Glass Elevator* is EXACTLY the length of time it takes to reach deep space, at a velocity of a **zillion kilometres per hour**.)

3 When you have reached **deep space**, select and play the love songs.

4 Glue the mirror to the rocket's outer wall.

) Wait.

6 **You might have to wait quite a while.**

When the **Vermicious Knid** sees itself in the mirror, it will be stunned by its own beauty and **FREEZE**!

8 Quickly whip out the net from its hiding place and plonk it right over the **Vermicious Knid**.

9 Fly back to **planet Earth**.

10 Take the shoebox to **London**, **England**.

11 Go to Buckingham Palace. Ask to see the **Queen**.

12 The Queen, who knows a lot about strange beings after her dealings with the **BFG**, will immediately invite you to afternoon tea. The Vermicious Knid, on the other hand, will be sent straight to London Zoo. **Job done.**

Answers

SPOT THE MISCHIEF-MAKER

Pages 29–30: It's WILLY WONKA from *Charlie and the Chocolate Factory* and *Charlie and the Great Glass Elevator*, of course!

Pages 36–37: Mr Fox from *Fantastic Mr Fox*.

Pages 52–53: Mrs Twit! Did you get it or are YOU a twit too?

Pages 72–73: George Kranky from *George's Marvellous Medicine*.

HOW MANY HAVE YOU READ?

☐ ☐ ☐ ☐ ☐

☐ ☐ ☐ ☐ ☐

☐ ☐ ☐ ☐ ☐

MORE THAN 5 WHOOPSY-SPLUNKERS! You've got some reading to do!

MORE THAN 10 More tremendous things await – keep turning those pages

ALL OF THEM? Whoopee! Which was your favourite?

STORIES ARE GOOD FOR YOU.

Roald Dahl said,
*'If you have good thoughts, they will shine
out of your face like sunbeams and you
will always look lovely.'*

We believe in doing good things.
That's why ten per cent of all Roald Dahl income*
goes to our charity partners. We have supported
causes including: specialist children's nurses, grants for
families in need, and educational outreach programmes.
Thank you for helping us to sustain this vital work.

Find out more at roalddahl.com